Beaver Yea

Books written and illustrated by IRENE BRADY

America's Horses & Ponies
A Mouse Named Mus
Beaver Year
Wild Mouse
Doodlebug
Elephants on the Beach
Wild Babies
Owlet, the Great Horned Owl

Books illustrated by IRENE BRADY

Five Fat Raccoons by Berniece Freschet
Forest Log by James Newton
Have You ever Heard of a Kangaroo Bird by Barbara Brenner
Animal Babysitters by Frances Zweifel
Rajpur, Last of the Bengal Tigers by Robert McClung
Gorilla by Robert McClung
Peeping in the Shell by Faith McNulty
Whitetail by Robert McClung
Lili, A Giant Panda of Sichuan by Robert McClung
Living Treasure by Laurence Pringle
Summer Bird Feeding by John V. Dennis
Twenty-five Hikes Along the Pacific Crest Trail by Don & Lolly Skillman

Beaver
Year

Written and illustrated by Irene Brady

Nature Works
Third Printing 1997
on ♻ paper
ISBN   0-915965-02-X

Library of Congress Cataloging in Publication Data

Brady, Irene.
  Beaver year.

  Summary: Chronicles the lives of two beavers from
the time they are born until they begin their own
family.
  1. Beavers—Legends and stories.
[1. Beavers—Fiction] I. Title.
PZ10.3.B728Be   [Fic]   75-38907
ISBN 0-915965-02-X

Many people helped me create this book. Tom Miller fanned the first sparks by sharing his shy beaver family during early pre-dawns on the river bank. As they swam and dived, towed green branches through the rippling water, and lived their lives as beavers always have, I watched entranced and sketched, absorbing the essence of what it's like to be a beaver.

Ginny Post lent her lake cabin for a long week of beaver observation and sketching from shore and canoe. Hope Sawyer Buyukmihci, who created the Unexpected Wildlife Refuge in Newfield, New Jersey, let me use her incomparable file of beaver photographs to illustrate beaver activities I was unable to sketch from life. Grace Henson, Jackie Miller, and Larry Kistler critiqued the artwork in progress. Sue and Earl were waiting at the finish line with a cold bottle of champagne. Many other people have, in large and small ways, cheered me on. Thank you, friends.

Beaver Year

CASSIE WAS BORN in the early morning. The first thing she felt was her mother's tongue and teeth and gentle furry fingers drying and cleaning her. The first sound her newborn beaver ears heard was her mother's soft crooning coo. Cassie's tiny mouth opened and her faint voice mewed into the dim gray light filtering through the top of the lodge. Her mother answered with soft oohs and ummms, eeeeuhs and eeeeoooooows, and whuffly snorts that sounded almost like words.

Cassie was comforted by her mother's voice and gentle grooming, and as her coat dried and fluffed out and her eyes began to focus, she gazed wide-eyed at everything around her.

Across the den, nearly six feet away, three yearlings stared at Cassie curiously. They were Cassie's three brothers, born the year before. They edged closer to get a better look at this tiny newcomer, but Cassie's mother warned them away with a grunt. Only a year before they had been Cassie's size — about as big as half-grown kittens — with fuzzy brown coats and tiny, downy paddle-tails. Now they were half as big as the mother beaver.

Soon Cassie was joined by Paddle, a new brother her own size. Growing hungry, they squealed their kittenlike cries. As soon as their mother had them all dried off and neat, she gathered them to the four teats between her front legs and curled around them protectively.

Outside the lodge, the late May sunshine was warm and pleasant. It warmed the stick-and-mud lodge in the middle of the beaver pond and sparkled off the water that trickled around the ends of the beaver dam.

In the marsh, a giant old beaver dug in the cattails. He was pulling up and eating the tender lower stalks and new pale leaves, which taste much like cucumbers. After a winter diet of tree bark and pond lily stems, the new green growth tasted delicious. Now, with a leaf still trailing from his mouth, the old beaver raised his head and listened. Mewing sounds! He'd heard that sound every year about this time! The new kits were here!

The old beaver clambered awkwardly into the watery channel cut through the marsh by some long ago beaver. On land he waddled, but in the water he moved gracefully and beautifully. He swam through the sunny water of the winding channel, which would lead him into the pond near the lodge.

Even though the outside of the lodge was hot, the room inside was dark and cool. The yearlings, the mother beaver and her newborn kits were clustered on a platform of sticks and sweet-smelling shredded cedar bark when suddenly the water heaved and splashed from one of the entrance tunnels in the floor and a giant dripping black shape lunged up beside them. The babies squealed and tried to burrow under their mother, but their mother

was not afraid. She had heard her mate enter the long under-water tunnel and had been expecting him. They exchanged some murmurs as he nuzzled the babies, then he sat back to dry and groom himself.

On the other side of the lodge, the three yearlings, bored already with the new kits, started a wrestling match. Soon they had scuffled and tumbled themselves to the edge of a plunge hole filled with water and plopped into it. With a last squeak and snort, they gulped breaths of air and dived, heading for the open water of the pond for a game of tag.

The yearlings still missed their four older sisters and brothers, the two-year-olds, who had left just a few days before to look for

their own homes and mates on other creeks and rivers. The two adults had lived and raised their families at this lodge for eight years, watching litter after litter of two-year-olds go off to make their own way in the world.

Beavers had lived in this lodge and pond for many years. The dam was about forty feet long and almost six feet high. Every beaver who had lived there had added more sticks and mud to make it stronger and higher and longer. There was a smaller dam above the main dam, but no beavers lived there.

Cassie and Paddle knew nothing about the dams and ponds yet. For the first few days they slept and nursed and mewed and explored the insides of the lodge. The lodge was big enough to hold fifteen beavers, which is about as many beavers as a colony ever has. The floor was divided into an eating platform and a sleeping platform. The beavers ate and groomed on the eating platform. The sleeping platform was built about six inches higher than the eating platform to keep it dry. It was made of a thick layer of wood shavings through which water could drain. Two plunge holes came up through the floor of the eating platform so that when the beavers ate they could just drop the chewed twigs into the holes.

There was plenty of room for the kits to play in the big lodge. On the fifth day, Cassie and Paddle were tumbling on the floor with fierce squeals and squeaks, shoving and tugging in a tiny battle, when they rolled into one of the plunge holes.

"EEEEEEEEEEUH! EEEEEEEEEEEE!" they screeched, and sneezed and thrashed around in the cold water. Their mother had been trying to nap on the sleeping platform, but at the first sound of frightened kits and splashing water she was on her feet and scrambling for the plunge hole. Swiftly, she leaned out and grabbed Paddle's tail in her teeth and dragged the squeaking kit out of the water. Then she reached for Cassie and boosted her up over the edge with her nose. She gathered the two wet babies to her, whimpering anxiously, and began to wipe and groom them. The kits weren't very wet. The water had not soaked through their fuzzy coats or wet them to the skin.

While the mother beaver was grooming Paddle, Cassie was sniffing and licking her own coat in great surprise. She had never paid much attention to her coat before. Now this damp, slick fur and wet tail and feet seemed to bring out her grooming instinct. Sitting on her tail, she started to comb and smooth her coat just the way adult beavers do, using the special split toenail on her fourth rear toe. She tried to groom her sides but she kept falling over. The mother beaver held Paddle between her paws as she rolled him and combed his fur carefully with her claws and long yellow teeth. When she had finished with him, she turned to Cassie. Even though the little kit was dry from her own grooming, her mother picked her up as she had Paddle, and, nuzzling oil

from the gland at the base of Cassie's tail, she finished the grooming job.

It takes a long time for kits to learn how to oil and fluff their coats well enough to keep them from getting soaked each time they go into the water. Paddle was beginning to snuffle his coat and make some grooming movements when Cassie sneaked up behind him and wrestled him into the pool again just for fun. Their mother pulled them out at once and again dried them off, but while she was grooming Cassie, Paddle jumped back into the pool for another try at this new game. It was then that their mother gave up and just sat and watched them, grabbing one now and then by the tail if it seemed in danger.

When the kits were only six days old and tried to dive, they were so light and fluffy that they couldn't get more than halfway under before they bobbed up again like corks. By the time they were ten days old, though, they had grown strong and heavy enough to swim down several inches and begin to explore the underwater tunnels.

The beavers were well equipped for living underwater. As soon as their heads went below the surface, their nostrils and ear flaps closed tight so that water could not come in. Clear membranes slid across their eyes to protect them from muddy water and floating sticks. Skin flaps closed off their mouths just behind their front teeth so that they could gnaw sticks without getting their mouths full of water.

When swimming, the beavers folded their front paws under their chins and kicked with their hind feet. They used their tails as rudders to change direction, or if they were in a big hurry they flapped them up and down to gain speed. Several times the kits got lost in the branching tunnels and their mother or father had to go looking for them.

When they were two weeks old, the kits were eating green leaves from branches their parents or the yearlings brought into the lodge. Later on they learned to hold twigs in their paws and turn them rapidly while chipping off and eating the bark with their teeth. Once in a while they would stop to grind their upper

teeth against their lower teeth to sharpen them, then they would go on eating.

The kits loved to groom. They would go up to the other beavers, touch noses, mew, and dance and whirl in front of them. This beaver signal meant, "I'll groom you if you'll groom me." Then they would spend many minutes combing and smoothing each other's fur.

For the first few weeks, the beaver kits had been trusting and fearless, but as time passed they became timid and were frightened by sudden noises, movements, or strange smells. They would race to hide or dive into the plunge holes at the slightest disturbance. This happens to all beaver kits about the time they

are ready to go outside the lodge. Until the kits gradually learn which things are false alarms and which are real, they are afraid of nearly everything. This probably saves their lives many times from hungry coyotes, wolverines, owls, hawks, osprey, bear, mink, cougars, wolves, and maybe even otters.

When Paddle and Cassie were about two months old, they were ready to go outside and see the world. They were still small — about the size of a small cat — and they weighed six or seven pounds each. For a week now they had been nursing less and less.

One morning their father woke up, stretched, and slipped down into the cool waters of the plunge hole, followed by the yearlings. The mother nudged the kits down after them and then dived in behind. When they surfaced outside in the deep water of the pond, the thick white mist was still rising from the water. Down on the pond bottom a rough-skinned newt shook the silt from its back and slowly rose to the surface for a breath of air. A trout came by and nibbled lightly on Paddle's tail.

On the sedge grasses overhanging the pond, the dragonflies spread their wings as the first rays of sunshine warmed their blood. A bat made one last swoop over the pond for a bedtime drink before starting his daylong sleep.

The father beaver clambered out onto the flat shelf of mud at the edge of the pond and sat on his tail to groom. The mother beaver climbed out beside him with the kits and yearlings crowd-

ing up beside her, shaking and grooming the water from their coats. When the old beaver was dry and shiny, he waddled up a trail and soon came back dragging a leafy aspen branch which he shared with the others.

When they were full, they all swam around the edges of the pond to inspect and add to what looked like mud patties on the rocks. The old beavers gathered mud from the pond edge and patted it onto the flat boulders. Then they crouched over the patties, kicked one hind leg, and squirted a sticky liquid on them from pouches beneath their tails. This liquid was called castoreum and smelled pleasant and strong. It marked the boundaries of the beaver pond. The kits copied the older beavers'

movements, but when they kicked, no castoreum came out. Their pouches were not yet developed. When the morning tour was finished, the beavers slid back into the water for a snack of pond algae, scooping it into their mouths with their paws.

SPLAT! Mother beaver's tail came down hard on the surface of the water, and after a great splashing of slapping tails there were no beavers to be seen. Looking up to the silver surface of the pond, the beavers on the pond bottom saw the shadow of an osprey drift over. Beavers have large lungs and can stay underwater for as long as fifteen minutes. After about three minutes, though, the beavers decided the danger was over and they had just surfaced again when one of the kits slapped an alarm. Once

more they dived into the water with a mighty splash. After a few minutes, the mother beaver went up to try to find the danger. She surfaced silently and looked in all directions.

There it was. The Danger. It looked like a great blue heron to the mother beaver and she circled it to make sure. Yes, that was it. She dove back down to where the youngsters waited and nudged them to the surface. The older beavers weren't afraid of the heron. It lived along the pond edge and often fished in the shallows for small fish and frogs. Since the heron didn't scare the older beavers, the kits began to learn by example which creatures were to be feared and which weren't.

Several times that day the kits gave the alarm. Once when a deer and fawn came silently to the pond . . . once when the pileated woodpecker flew cackling across the water . . . and once when an otter family glided over the dam and into the pond. The older beavers knew the otter family well and often shared the pond with them. The cubs and kits soon made the pond ring with splashes, yips, and chirps. The old beavers just went about their work.

Sometimes otters hunt and kill beaver kits. Perhaps this only happens if they cannot find any other food. These otters had never bothered the beavers, so they all lived peaceably together. After about an hour the otters wandered off upstream.

At the dam, the father beaver was trying to plug a leak that was

trickling through the mud and twigs at a low spot. With the curious kits trailing him, he dived to the bottom of the pond and dug up an armload of mud and sticks. Pressing them to his chest and chin with the backs of his forepaws, he swam back to the dam. Rising on his hind feet with a grunt, he carried the armload up the steep side of the dam and dumped it in a heap where the water trickled. Then he patted and tamped down the mud and sticks with his forepaws and chin, sealing the hole.

As the father worked, the kits dug in the mud, too, but they didn't yet know what to do with the mud they stirred up, so they started a game of tag, flashing through the water with a smooth grace they never had on land.

As the sun slipped below the mountain ridge and the evening darkness seeped into the valley, the night sounds of the marsh began. Frogs hiccupped and chirped, a great horned owl hooted softly from farther back in the woods, and seven sleepy beavers made soft rippling V's as they swam across the pond to the lodge and bed.

This small beaver family had never seen humans, so they felt safe to eat and play and work in the daytime as all beavers once did. Where humans disturb the stillness of the wilderness, beavers hide during the day and come out only when it grows dark.

By the time late summer arrived, the kits knew many things. Instinct is important in a beaver's life and some things, like dam

building and food storing, are instinctive, not learned. But experience does help a lot. Little by little, the kits learned the best way to carry a stick in their mouths and how to poke it into the mud of the dam to mend a leak. They now knew how to plaster the dam and lodge to prepare for winter. Helping the big beavers, they climbed up the sides of the lodge with armloads of mud to make it warm and strong against winter snow, cold, and predators.

The beavers plastered mud all over the lodge except for the very top. Here at the tip no mud would be placed, for it was here that clean fresh air poured down past sticks and twigs during the cold winter so that the beavers would always have lots of air. It was here that steam from the beavers' breath and warm bodies would rise and keep snow and ice from freezing over the air hole.

When they weren't plastering and dam mending, the beavers felled trees and gathered leafy branches for the winter food supply. The kits couldn't cut trees yet. In fact, the yearlings were just now learning. The old beavers could cut a tree two or three feet thick, but most of the trees they chose were six to ten inches thick. Then they cut them up into lengths that could be scooted down the channels into the pond and either used on the dam or put into the food supply near the lodge. The kits could carry small branches, the yearlings could handle saplings. With the work of all the beavers there was soon a big tangle of branches and twigs in the pond next to the lodge. This would be enough food for them to eat during the winter.

Then, like a cold, still blanket, winter came to the pond. Snow fell in giant flakes and covered all the trees and shrubs and the dam and lodge. Each night seemed colder than the last and the water cooled steadily. Some water beetles still swam in the chill water. Most of the birds had flown south with the first frost, although some ducks still paddled about in the shallows eating the last of the summer water plants. The garter snake which had rippled across the pond all summer coiled itself tightly into its hole in the beaver lodge and drifted into a long winter sleep. Down at the bottom of the pond the frogs and turtles and newts lay buried deep in the mud, still as mummies. Only spring could bring them to life again.

One night in October, the lodge crackled and groaned with cold and when the beavers woke up the next morning, the pond was frozen over. The kits, who followed their father out into the pond, were astonished when their fuzzy noses found the ice like a lid on the pond.

Their father bumped his nose on the underside of the ice, testing its strength. He finally dived to the bottom of the pond, and then, gaining speed, he swam straight up at the ice. His front paws were folded under his chin, his eyes were tightly closed, and his head was pulled far down between his shoulders to make a good battering ram.

CRUNCH! The ice cracked and heaved and the head and shoulders of the wet black beaver surged above the ice. He swam around the edge of the hole he had made, bringing his chin down hard on the ice to break off chips and make the hole bigger. Every day, now, and sometimes more often, he would come out to make sure his hole stayed open. It was good to have a place to get out. Sometimes for a change of diet one of the beavers would waddle across the ice into the forest for fresh twigs, but it was dangerous out there and their feet and tails might freeze. They never stayed out on the ice long.

That winter a red fox circled the pond each day as he patrolled the marsh for voles and mice. Owls often flew over in the frozen night to grab any small animal that stirred below, for even in winter a marsh is full of life. The pileated woodpecker made the snowy woods ring with his hammering search for insects in old trees.

In their strong lodge the beavers were comfortable. A wolverine often galloped across the ice of the pond to climb up to the top of the lodge and breathe deeply the warm, delicious beaver scent rising through the top hole. When they heard him, all the beavers inside would fall silent and huddle together, barely breathing while the hungry hunter snuffled and sometimes tore at the sticks and mud. But the beavers had done their job well.

The frozen mud was like iron and held the sticks tightly. Still, the beavers always dreaded his step and the rotten-meat breath that came whuffling down through the hole.

The first signs of spring for the beavers were the slushing up and finally the melting away of the ice. Once more they could dive and swim in the open water of the pond. Even the old beavers could sometimes be persuaded to play a little game of tag. The willows were putting out tiny green buds and new marsh grasses were poking up through the mud when disaster struck.

High up in the mountains above the beaver pond one warm spring night a cloudburst came. Gigantic piles of dark, rain-filled

clouds gathered around the mountain peaks and poured torrents of rain upon the mountainsides. Within moments the mountains were covered with sheets of running water. It couldn't soak in because the ground was already full of melted snow water, so it drained off down the mountain meadows to join the already flooding creeks.

The rising water cut into steep creek banks and washed boulders that had been covered for millions of years out into the swift-running water. Within a few hours the thundering, rushing water had swirled into the small pool just above the beaver pond. With a crackle of snapping branches, it broke the little dam at the pool's end and gushed into the big pond with a sudden roar.

The beavers, just waking in the early spring dawn, were taken by surprise. In one short minute their pond changed from a still, calm pool into a turmoil of muddy water and slashing, whirling sticks and branches. The water rose inside the lodge until the beavers were standing in water up to their bellies. Frantically, the two old beavers dived down the exit holes, only to be met at the ends with clashing, sharp-pointed sticks that jabbed and clutched at them. They turned in panic and kicked back up the tunnels to the flooded platform.

The swirling waters were tearing at the ancient lodge, and it rocked and swung crazily in the water, which was now pouring in through a gap in the side. Suddenly, with a deep groan of breaking branches, the lodge ripped free from the pond bed and was flung against the dam by the rushing water. The dam and lodge both broke open with the shock, and the lodge filled with choking muddy water.

Each beaver was fighting for its life, and the yearlings were first to claw their way out of the broken lodge. They scrambled up onto the dam and rushed along its crest to find safety on the bank of the pond. Their mother scrambled onto the dam next, then turned to reach for the kits. But it was too late.

Just as she turned, the other side of the dam gave way and the broken lodge, with Paddle, Cassie, and the father beaver still clinging to it, went splashing into the muddy floodwaters. Gasping and choking, the three beavers clung tightly to the lodge,

which was now only a raft of sticks carrying them downstream. All of a sudden it hit a snag and rushing water whipped it to the shore. The big beaver was flung into the willows, but as he scrambled to his feet the water once more grabbed the raft with the two little beavers still clinging tightly to it and carried them away downstream.

For a while the old beaver scrambled after them, but he couldn't go very fast through the thickets of willow and alder on the banks, and at last he turned sadly back upstream to look for the rest of his family and his mate. Together they would rebuild the lodge and dam. The yearlings, now almost two years old, would be leaving in a few weeks. And already the seeds of a new family

were stirring in his mate. The old beaver plodded wearily up the canyon toward home.

All through the day the kits rode their raft through forests and echoing mountain canyons. They hung on to each other, whimpering and crying. They were terribly afraid to stay on the shrinking raft, but they were more afraid of trying to get to shore by plunging into the muddy water full of giant tree trunks and thundering, rolling boulders. It was almost dusk when a passing tree finally nudged them ashore on a sloping bank of gravel and sand. They had just enough time to force their trembling legs to carry them onto the little beach before the tree swung around, brushed their raft out into the stream, and sank it.

Shaking and wailing, they dragged themselves across the gravel and into a thicket of willows. As the sun dropped below the mountain crest, the two kits calmed a little. Stopping often to touch noses and whimper to each other, they groomed their drenched coats until they were once again fluffy and dry.

Paddle and Cassie were almost yearlings. In one more month, if they had stayed with their parents, they would have seen the birth of the new litter of kits. Yearling beavers sometimes wander away from home to explore and see new places. A few even leave permanently to begin new dams and dens during their first year. But it doesn't happen very often, and Paddle and Cassie hadn't chosen to come exploring. Now they had to succeed or they would not live through the summer.

The first and most important thing was to find a place to live. Together they wandered for almost two months and nearly fifteen miles before they came to a place that looked as though it would do. The two beavers, now yearlings, had stayed close together through their long trip, traveling and sleeping side by side along stream banks and in thickets. Paddle and Cassie, as often happens between brother and sister beavers from the same litter, had chosen each other as mates. Even if they had left home as two-year-olds they very likely would have chosen to leave together to start a colony.

They finally found their idea of a fine place to make a home. It was a sparkling stream, lying in a wide rocky and sandy stream

bed, with willows and aspens lining it on both sides. They wandered up and down its banks, leaving little mud patties sprinkled with castoreum where they explored.

Beavers make two kinds of homes — dens and lodges. If there is a bank, they often dig a den right into it. But if the stream bank is too low, they pile a stack of sticks in the middle of the pond, then tunnel into it and dig out a cavity inside. The stream Cassie and Paddle had chosen had a high bank, so they dug a den.

The yearlings had never built a dam from scratch before, but they seemed to agree on the place to make it -- a place where water trickled noisily between some rocks. Whenever they

stopped to eat, they carried their peeled sticks to the dam to make it higher. In some places they lifted and carried rocks from the stream bottom to lengthen and strengthen the dam. In fact, almost half of their dam was made of stones. Soon a small pond formed.

A few yards upstream there was an aspen thicket where Cassie and Paddle cut saplings. They pulled and floated the little trees, still with twigs and leaves on them, through the pond to the dam, where they jabbed them into the stream bed to anchor them. Then, digging up armloads of mud and rocks, they pressed them against any part of the dam that leaked. Bit by bit, the mud and leaves began to clog the dam and make it leakproof. Slowly

the pond became still and deep with plenty of room for Cassie and Paddle to hide on the bottom and to cover the entrance to their bank den with several inches of water.

The young beavers enlarged their den until it was big enough for two beavers. It was now three feet across and almost a foot high, with a broad sleeping platform and two plunge holes in the floor. One hole led almost straight out into the pond, but the other twisted and branched and came out farther from the den.

Gathering the winter food supply was easy around this new pond. They didn't have to go far. Paddle and Cassie were still only half-grown, about eighteen pounds each, but they were big enough to cut small aspens, willows, and alders, so they cut the ones closest to the pond borders. Since most of the trees had heavier branches on the side nearer the water and naturally leaned that way, the trees usually fell with a noisy smack into the water. It was easy, then, for the yearlings to tow them to a spot near the den door and anchor them to the stream bottom.

The water of the pond grew cooler as the days became shorter, keeping the branches and leaves of their food supply from spoiling or rotting. They were prepared for winter when it came.

Through the long winter days and nights in the bank den, Paddle and Cassie groomed each other and cooed and talked with the special sounds that courting beavers make.

One night in January, Cassie swam slowly out into the dark water under the ice and Paddle followed. There, in a swirl of

silver bubbles and dancing waves they mated and began their family. And when the buds on the trees swelled and tightened with spring life, Cassie, too, grew big with young.

Paddle was with her when the kits were born, although he kept his distance across the den. Cassie bore two wiggly kits, and as she cleaned and dried them for the first time, holding them in her paws and combing their short fuzz with her teeth and tongue, she felt Paddle beside her in the darkness. Their noses came together in a quick, tender beaver greeting, and as she lay down to nurse the tiny mewling kits he sat proudly protective on her other side. Warm and close, a good family, they were the tiny beginning of a new beaver colony.